捕捉

感傷

賀星◎著

冷月啊　　我已醉
一盞天燈孤零飄搖

序

在價值觀混淆的時候，人會
變得健忘，我只能試著捕捉
一些感傷………

Preface

When values become confused,

People become forgetful.

I can   Only try to capture some sorrow

………

目錄

目錄

Contents

領帶

....

也曾揣摩這條領帶
體會臨別贈予的氣息
花色及圖案
是否暗示難說的心意
銀亮的領夾
也看不出一絲絲絕決
猜想你的眼神
寧願保持原來的情景

Necktie

Out of the necktie I still
Sense the tinge of farewell.
Do the colors and design
Hide your secret intention?
Yet the tie clip doesn't
Reveal any bit of the coldest.
I guess you still wish your eyes
Could tell the story of the past.

心動

錯身而過的瞬間
我們竟已完成傾訴
陌生的身軀
在暫停的時空顫動

眼神忽然綻放
不再矜持的喜悅
或許為了補償
隱約殘留的期待

Being Moved

The moment we passed by each other,
We are already intimately familiar.
The strange body is shivering in
This transient space-time.

In an instant the eyes are blooming
With unstrained joy,
Maybe in compensation

For looming expectations.

板橋車站

夜車在板橋車站甦醒
並沒看見熟悉的身影
夜車在板橋車站離開
仍然留下些微的嘆息
月台燈光蒼白
零落旅客昏沈
還是找不到
遺失在火車站的舊情

Panchiao Railway Station

When it awoke at the Panchiao
    railway station,
The night train perceived no familiars.
When it left the Panchiao Station,
The night train was lightly sighing.
The pale light on the platform
Shed over the lonely drowsy passengers,
Who found no lost emotions at the
    railway station.

訊息

　手機劇烈顫動
　傳送渴望的訊息
　輕聲細語
　來自壓抑許久的思念
　雖然不是深夜
　也帶來一點哀傷

A message

The mobile phone throbs violently,
Bringing a message of desire
In a light and gentle voice,
That is the longing long withheld.
Although not late at night,
There is still a bit of distress in it.

一絲白髮

烏黑長髮裏面
隱藏著一絲白髮
年輕活潑的笑容
有些不為人知的哀愁
遇見相像的少女
總又想起那絲白髮

One Gray Strand

Wrapped in the jet black hair

Is a strand of gray hair,

Hidden in the young and lively smile.

Is some sadness not perceived by others?

When facing a girl

I can think of nothing but that single strand.

思念

眼神消失於電扶梯之後
仍遺留妳的身形及臉龐
可能是殘餘的時空影像
也可能是源於意志超能
我們不經意的共振
產生無限延長的思緒
如果能量不變不滅
於觸碰之後才能淡忘

Missing

I cast my eyes behind the escalator
Where your figure and face can still be
    traced.
Perhaps it is the remnant of the temporal
    and spatial image,
Perhaps it has originated from the super
    power to will.
The casual resonance between us
Will produce boundless thinking.
If this energy is always kept in balance,
Nothing will be forgotten before
    our next meeting.

重逢

磁波的感應仍在
中斷的訊息再度連接
從來沒有絕緣體
能阻止將發生的戀情
因為是亙古的引力
與沒有邊界的思念
只怕重逢相擁
引發無盡的連鎖反應

Meeting Again

The influence of the magnetism still exist,
While the broken message is reconnected.
Never will an insulator withhold
The coming outburst of loving emotion.
For it is the everlasting attraction
And that missing feeling without limit.
What I am only concerned about is
The long-lasting embrace that will bring
 an endless chain reaction.

情人夜

將暗戀藏入手機
成為數位化的簡訊
向遠方傳遞
尚未發酵的愛情
或向宇宙表達
沒有實體的情慾

冷月啊　我已醉
一盞天燈孤零飄搖

On the Night of the Valentine's Day

I input my hidden love in the mobile phone,
Translating it into a digital message,
And send it far away.
Neither unfermented love
nor the expression of the Universe
Possess the unsubstantial passion.

Oh, cold moon, I am drunk,
Like a heaven lamp tottering alone.

婚宴的迷思

迷失於敦化北路
尋找妳婚宴的地點
紛亂的思緒
導致無意識地排徊
停在十字路口抽煙
微風移動路樹車流
唉　就是故意遺忘
也不能證明些什麼

Confused Reflection on the Wedding Dinner

Lost on the Dumhua North Road,
I am looking for a restaurant to hold
    your wedding dinner.
With a disarrayed mind,
I am wandering from place to place.
Finally finding myself smoking at the
    crossroads,
The roadside trees are flowing in the
    breeze.
Oh, even if I am intending to forget,
It cannot prove anything.

羅東之夜

　　冷清的街景
　　在寒夜中停格
　　堤樹之外暗淡
　　是沒有止境的無奈
　　啊　寂寞羅東
　　夜照酒館舞動
　　我的肢體凌亂
　　啊　酒醉羅東
　　手機伴我入夢
　　思念已經失控

The Night of Luotung

The bleak street is
Frozen in the cold night.
There is only darkness beyond the bank
of trees,
And boundless hesitation
Oh, lonely Luotung
Souls Tice pub is dancing,
While my limbs flail about.
Oh, drunken Luotung
The mobile phone sends me into a dream;
My thoughts are also out of control.

夜歌

端午之夜
小酒館冷清
老板娘哀淒地吟唱
似已觸動許多往事
只好乾了一杯
用來阻止淚珠
啊　冰涼的啤酒
洗不淨我的胸腔
莫非也需藉一曲悲歌
來訴說委屈不平的際遇

Night Song

On the night of the Dragonboat Festival,
In a bleak pub, the landlady
Was humming a melancholy song,
    stirring up many a bygone era.
I can not but empty my cup
to withhold the tears.
Oh, even the cool beer
Can not cleanse my heart.
Perhaps I also need a sad melody
To pour out the unfair treatment of me.

餞別

曙光未現
寒風吹斜燈影
快上車罷
別在錢櫃門前停留
難道飲酒與高歌
還沒完全表達心意
這條陌生的馬路
不知即將通往何處

A Farewell Dinner

Before the dawn,
The chilly wind is playing
   with the lamp shadow.
Get on the taxi,
Do not loiter before the Cashbox.
Can the booze and sharp song
   not fully express my mind?
I am wondering, where this
   strange road is leading now?

市場乞者

熟悉的面孔
在攤子與布棚間覓食
烈日焚燒嘈雜人聲
汗水滲刺眼角
剩下的身軀與錄音帶
是向天促銷的本錢
磨擦地面的傷口
是每日必經的劇痛
只有化緣和尚漫步
叮叮鈴聲帶來清涼

A Beggar in the Market

The familiar face is begging
Among the stalls and canopies.
The burning sun is scorching the chaos,
The sweat is penetrating into the
    corners of the eyes.
Only the body and records are left for
    promoting to the heavens.
The wounds that rub the ground
Strongly stab the body every day.
Only the alms-begging monks that
    walk by
Can bring some coolness, with their
    ringing bells.

陳酒

只有金門高粱
共赴隨興的邀約
這種家常小館
竟能烹調舊時風味
笑容已經掩過疲憊
不再常有歡聚情景
還是放量喝罷
陳酒方能道盡交情

Old Wine

There is no free chat over a get-together
Without Chin-Men Kaoliang spirit.
A small homelike tavern like this,
How can it cook the flavor of the past?
The smiles are hiding tiredness.
This scene of happy meeting is seldom
    seen now.
Let us drink our fill,
Friendship can be fully enveloped
    only in the old wine.

午睡

陽台盆栽落漠
視線從被角糢糊
或許迷夢之中
能夠重組纏綿情節
昏沉玻璃窗外
稀稀疏疏地下雨

Taking a Nap

Lonely finds the potted plant on the
    balcony,
Misty are the eyes peeping out of the
    corner of the quilt.
Perhaps in the daydreams
Are replayed those lingering scenes.
Out of the dullish windows
The rain is dripping--every now and
    then.

風雨

酒杯空懸吧台
桌椅沉默無語
並以爵士音符
構思一幅靜物畫
或許是風雨的關係
窗外樹葉抖動
或許是風雨的關係
沒人聊到天明

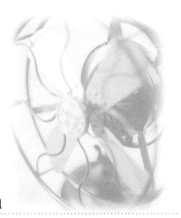

Wind and Rain

Empty is the cup on the bar counter,
Speechless are the chairs and tables.
With the jazz notes
    I am painting a still life.
Perhaps due to the wind and the rain,
The leaves of the tree out the window
    are shivering.
Perhaps due to the wind and rain,
No one is going to chat to morning light.

遊行

暗雲浮在人群臉上
車輛橫躺街頭對談
擴音器陣陣吶喊
呼喚著秋天的悲涼
隊伍已過十字路口
邁向凱達格蘭大道

The Procession

The faces of the pedestrians are
    darkly clouded,
The vehicles are lying on the street
    conversing.
From the loudspeakers come the
    continuous slogans,
Breathing out the melancholy autumn.
The procession has passed the
    crossroads,
Marching towards Ketagalan Avenue.

七條通

秋月冰涼
路邊燈影稀微
小酒館默默等待
行人路過的長巷
何時歡唱三更
已成沒有慾望的城市

The Seventh Avenue

The autumn moonlight is cool,
The roadside lamps are sparse.
The small tavern is silently waiting,
When will the long alley the
    pedestrians pass by
Be resounding with carols in the
    night?
In this city without desire.

觀棋

濃密的樹葉
把陽光篩落滿地
池塘圍繞涼亭
微風輕撫水紋
下棋的老者
討論著勝負策略
這座小型公園
是人生最後的戰場

Watching the Chess Game

The dense leaves of the trees
Are filtering the sunlight onto the
    ground.
A pavilion is located in the midst
    of the pond
Where the breeze is dabbing the waves.
There are two old men who are
    playing chess,
Discussing strategies for victory.
This small park has become
The last battlefield for them.

伴奏

燭光微微映照

桌桌客人的身影

煙味已經侵蝕

快要喝醉的酒吧

琴師隱約表白心意

主角是台上唱歌的人

The Accompaniment

The candlelight is lightly shining upon
The backs of the customers at the tables.
The smoke has immersed the pub
And drinks that have yet to be drunk.
The pianist's hidden mind seems to run
    like this,
The singer on the stage is the only
    protagonist.

中秋夜思

微涼的氣息
流動擴散著溫馨
因為愛在路邊燒烤
紅炭點燃著親情
無數人間煙火
供奉著一輪明月
啊　月光
撫摸著流落在外的人
也撫摸夜色中的家鄉

Reflections on Mid-Autumn Festival

In the cool breath of wind
Is flowing and spreading gentleness.
On the roadside is burning love,
The emotion of kinship has already
    kindled.
Smoke from the kitchen fires of the world
Are circling around the bright moon.
Oh, moon light
Is caressing the wandering people
While the hometown is in the shadows.

北投捷運

　　山巒銜接天空
　　已成捷運站的布景
　　因為不知方向
　　竟然在此面臨抉擇
　　轉乘新北投也好
　　或許要返回台北
　　又有一班列車離去
　　我似乎已忘了前程

Beitou Subway Station

The subway station is set
Against the mountains, stretching to
    heaven.
I don't know where I am heading for,
And here I have to decide
Whether to take the new Beitou subway,
    or return to Taipei.
As another train leaves
I seem to have forgotten where I am going.

沙魚煙攤

　　黃昏夜色漸濃
　　沙魚煙攤燈下
　　食客的背影
　　好像已坐了幾十年
　　傳統的醬料
　　古早的重慶北路

The Salted Sandfish stall

The eventide is denser and denser
Under the lamp of the salted sandfish
    stall.
Viewed from behind
The diners seem to have been sitting there
    for decades.
Enjoining the traditional sauce
On the age-old Chongqing North Road.

離愁

耶誕夜短暫相聚
又從機場來電告別
總有不捨的情義
離愁由飛機尾端消散
台北氣候已涼
或許上海更冷一些

The Melancholy Parting

After the transient get-together on
Christmas Eve,
I received a goodbye in the airport.
Mixed with reluctance,
When sadness is dissipated from the tail.
It has been cool in Taipei,
Maybe it is even colder in Shanghai.

透明銀幕

在捷運車尾觀賞
有關都市大樓的影片
捷運站逐漸縮小
四周景物跟著擴大
透過玻璃車窗
展現Zoom Out的技巧
暫時停格之後
又上演同樣的戲碼

The Transparent Screen

Watching a film about the
  skyscrapers in the metropolis.
At the end of the subway car,
The grandeur of the subway station
  diminishes,
While the things around are enlarged.
Through the glass window,
I am demonstrating the technique of
  Zooming Out.
After the temporary freeze frame,
The same play is performed again.

日月潭

欄杆連接深夜
陽台對飲到天明
遠方山形沉靜
潭水昏昏欲睡
何必再談論
塵世中的因果

每喝酒醉
就想到日月潭

Sun Moon Lake

Deep into the night by the balustrade
On the balcony two men drink till dawn.
In the distance the hills are still,
And the water in the lake is dozing off.
It is useless now to talk about
Cause and effect in this mundane world.

Each time I am drunk,
I will remember Sun Moon Lake.

慈聖宮

　　樹蔭掉落盤中
　　用歲月來佐酒
　　路邊攤料理
　　大稻埕碼頭的傳統
　　媽祖娘娘護祐
　　在廣場飲食的眾生

The Tsusheng Temple

The tree shade drops into the plate,
The years accompany the drinking.
The foods at the roadside stalls
Inherit the tradition of the Da-Dou-Cheng
    dock.
May Matsu bless
The crowd dining on the square.

鄉愁

飛機經過嘉義
窗外團團白雲
家園就在地面
歸路婉轉遙長
還沒抵達高雄
鄉愁已在空中發生

Homesickness

As the plane flies over Chiayi,
There are clouds all round.
The hometown is directly on the
    ground beneath,
The returning path begins to extend
    and wind.
Before I arrive in Kaohsiung,
I am already terribly homesick.

黑長大衣

佇立於捷運電扶梯
出口是快甦醒的星期一
為了寒冷的冬季
為了站外埋伏的紛擾
穿著堅強的黑長大衣
並以眼神武裝雕像的臉龐
美麗又勇敢的女子
陌生的從我身邊流過

The Black Overcoat

Standing by the subway escalator
The pretty courageous girl
Is heading for the exit of Monday that is
    soon waking.
Having in mind the wintry season,
Having in mind the hidden tumult
    outside the station,
She is clothed in a firm black overcoat,
Carving her face with the expression of
    her own eyes.
The strange now flits by me suddenly.

祭拜

牌位間起陣冷風
一支細香代表心意
陰陽交界徘徊
請不必留戀牽掛
往事浮現眼前
哀傷是暫時的感觸
軀殼已完全損壞
終於再也不必操勞

The Ceremony of Offering Sacrifice

Gusts of cold wind are blowing among
    the memorial tablets,
A branch of incense is uttering my regards.
Hovering between the boundaries of
    Yin and Yang,
There is nothing to care for.
When the past comes into our minds,
We will bemoan them for a while.
Since your body has been completely ruined.
There is nothing to take care of any more.

老歌

不經意打開電視
是媽媽愛聽的老歌
其中有許多故事
從年輕到老的辛酸
很想告訴媽媽
同時來觀賞回味
我在台北流淚
還是沒有拿起電話

An Old Song

An old song my mom loves came
From the TV I switched off casually.
Within the song are many stories that
Recall my memory of my mom,
From her youth to old age.
I wish to call my mom,
To come and talk with me.
But I just cry here in Taipei,
Without making the call.

國家圖書館出版品預行編目

捕捉感傷 / 賀星著. -- 一版. -- 臺北市：秀

威資訊科技, 2004[民 93]

　　面；　　公分. -- (語言文學類；PG0023)

　　ISBN 978-986-7614-54-4(平裝)

851.486　　　　　　　　　　93017689

語言文學類　PG0023

補捉感傷

編　　者 / 賀星
發 行 人 / 宋政坤
執行編輯 / 李坤城
圖文排版 / 莊芯媚
封面設計 / 莊芯媚
數位轉譯 / 徐真玉　沈裕閔
圖書銷售 / 林怡君
法律顧問 / 毛國樑　律師
出版印製 / 秀威資訊科技股份有限公司
　　　　　　台北市內湖區瑞光路 583 巷 25 號 1 樓
　　　　　　電話：02-2657-9211　　　傳真：02-2657-9106
　　　　　　E-mail：service@showwe.com.tw
經 銷 商 / 紅螞蟻圖書有限公司
　　　　　　台北市內湖區舊宗路二段 121 巷 28、32 號 4 樓
　　　　　　電話：02-2795-3656　　　傳真：02-2795-4100
　　　　　　http://www.e-redant.com

2004 年 10 月 BOD 一版
定價：150 元

讀 者 回 函 卡

感謝您購買本書，為提升服務品質，煩請填寫以下問卷，收到您的寶貴意見後，我們會仔細收藏記錄並回贈紀念品，謝謝！

1.您購買的書名：＿＿＿＿＿＿＿＿＿＿＿＿＿＿＿＿

2.您從何得知本書的消息？

　　□網路書店　□部落格　□資料庫搜尋　□書訊　□電子報　□書店

　　□平面媒體　□ 朋友推薦　□網站推薦　□其他＿＿＿＿＿

3.您對本書的評價：(請填代號　1.非常滿意 2.滿意 3.尚可 4.再改進)

　　封面設計＿＿　版面編排＿＿　內容＿＿　文/譯筆＿＿　價格＿＿

4.讀完書後您覺得：

　　□很有收獲　□有收獲　□收獲不多　□沒收獲

5.您會推薦本書給朋友嗎？

　　□會　□不會，為什麼？＿＿＿＿＿＿＿＿＿＿＿＿＿＿＿＿

6.其他寶貴的意見：＿＿＿＿＿＿＿＿＿＿＿＿＿＿＿＿＿＿

＿＿＿＿＿＿＿＿＿＿＿＿＿＿＿＿＿＿＿＿＿＿＿＿＿＿

＿＿＿＿＿＿＿＿＿＿＿＿＿＿＿＿＿＿＿＿＿＿＿＿＿＿

＿＿＿＿＿＿＿＿＿＿＿＿＿＿＿＿＿＿＿＿＿＿＿＿＿＿

讀者基本資料

姓名：＿＿＿＿＿＿＿＿＿　年齡：＿＿＿　性別：□女 □男

聯絡電話：＿＿＿＿＿＿＿　E-mail：＿＿＿＿＿＿＿＿＿

地址：＿＿＿＿＿＿＿＿＿＿＿＿＿＿＿＿＿＿＿＿＿＿＿

學歷：□高中(含)以下　　□高中　　□專科學校　　□大學

　　　□研究所(含)以上 □其他＿＿＿＿＿＿＿

職業：□製造業 □金融業 □資訊業 □軍警 □傳播業 □自由業

　　　□服務業 □公務員 □教職　□學生 □其他＿＿＿＿＿

To：114

台北市內湖區瑞光路 583 巷 25 號 1 樓

秀威資訊科技股份有限公司　　　收

寄件人姓名：

寄件人地址：□□□

(請沿線對摺寄回,謝謝!)

秀威與 BOD

BOD（Books On Demand）是數位出版的大趨勢，秀威資訊率先運用 POD 數位印刷設備來生產書籍，並提供作者全程數位出版服務，致使書籍產銷零庫存，知識傳承不絕版，目前已開闢以下書系：

一、BOD 學術著作—專業論述的閱讀延伸
二、BOD 個人著作—分享生命的心路歷程
三、BOD 旅遊著作—個人深度旅遊文學創作
四、BOD 大陸學者—大陸專業學者學術出版
五、POD 獨家經銷—數位產製的代發行書籍

BOD 秀威網路書店：www.showwe.com.tw
政府出版品網路書店：www.govbooks.com.tw

永不絕版的故事・自己寫・永不休止的音符・自己唱